The Ruby Princess and the Baby Dragon

READ MORE BOOKS ABOUT
THE JEWEL KINGDOM

1 ● The Ruby Princess Runs Away

2 ● The Sapphire Princess
Meets a Monster

3 ● The Emerald Princess
Plays a Trick

4 ● The Diamond Princess
Saves the Day

5 ● The Ruby Princess Sees a Ghost

6 ● The Sapphire Princess
Hunts for Treasure

7 ● The Emerald Princess Finds a Fairy

8 ● The Diamond Princess and the Magic Ball

Super Special 1: The Jewel Princesses and the
Missing Crown

THE JEWEL KINGDOM

The Ruby Princess and the Baby Dragon

JAHNNA N. MALCOLM

Illustrations by Neal McPheeters

SCHOLASTIC INC.
NEW YORK   TORONTO   LONDON   AUCKLAND   SYDNEY
MEXICO CITY   NEW DELHI   HONG KONG

ISBN 0-590-97877-2

12 11 10 9 8 7 6 5 4 3 2 1   8 9/9 0 1 2 3/0

Printed in the U.S.A.   40
First Scholastic printing, November 1998

For
Karen and Walter
and
their Royal Family:
Andrew, Michael, Helga, and Peter

CONTENTS

The Ruby Princess and the Baby Dragon

THE JEWEL KINGDOM

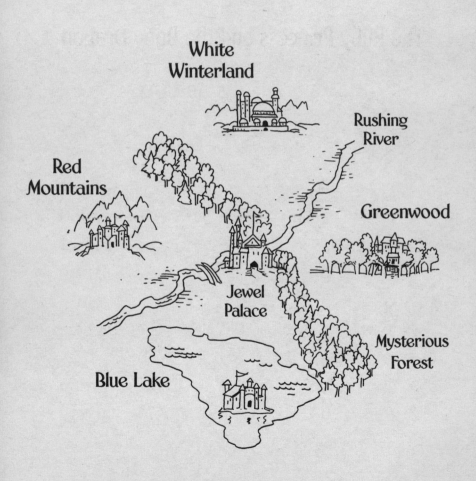

White
Winterland

Rushing
River

Red
Mountains

Greenwood

Jewel
Palace

Mysterious
Forest

Blue Lake

Roxanne Finds an Egg

"Only one more cottage to go," the Ruby Princess called as she skipped up to a tiny red door. "Hurry, Hapgood! Bring the basket."

"Coming, Princess!" a deep voice answered.

The voice belonged to a huge green Dragon with red-tipped wings. He carried a straw basket filled with fruit and nuts in his big Dragon jaws.

Princess Roxanne and Hapgood had spent the afternoon delivering Friendship Baskets to the creatures of the Red Mountains. It was Roxanne's idea. It was a nice thing to do for her people.

Hapgood joined the princess at the little door.

"This is so much fun," Roxanne said to her closest friend and advisor. "I just love surprising people."

Roxanne fluffed her thick black hair, smoothed her long red velvet dress, then tapped on the door. Moments later a Gnome with a long gray beard opened it.

"Princess Roxanne!" the Gnome cried with delight. "What a pleasant surprise!"

"Hello, Applesap!" Roxanne giggled as she gave him a hug. "I've missed you."

Roxanne had met Applesap and his wife, Marigold, on the day Roxanne was crowned the Ruby Princess. Together they had fought her kingdom's enemies, the Darklings. From that day forward they were good friends.

Applesap rushed out to greet Hapgood, then called over his shoulder, "Marigold! Drop what you're doing and come see our friends!"

There was a loud crash in the kitchen, and a round-faced Gnome with bright red hair scurried out the door.

"Oh, my stars!" Marigold cried, clapping her chubby hands together. "If it isn't the princess and that wonderful old fire-breather, Hapgood!"

Marigold kissed Roxanne and stood on tiptoe to hug Hapgood. "How long has it been?" she asked.

"Too long," Roxanne replied. "At least a month."

"Then you haven't met Peaches," Applesap said. "Peaches is our new kitten."

"A kitten?" Roxanne cried. "Oh, please let me see her!"

While Marigold brought them cups of warm honey mead, Applesap introduced Roxanne and Hapgood to the new pet.

Peaches was an orange-colored ball of fur with white whiskers, yellow eyes, and little white paws.

"Mew! Mew!" she squeaked.

Roxanne cuddled Peaches in her arms for the entire visit. When it was time to leave, it was hard for the princess to give her up. "She is such a darling kitten," Roxanne said. "I want to hold her forever."

"Anytime you want to play with her,

come visit," Applesap said. "You are always welcome in our home."

After they said good-bye to their Gnome friends, Hapgood and Roxanne walked back to a small wooden wagon. They had been using it to deliver the baskets.

"You liked that kitten, didn't you?" the Dragon asked.

Roxanne nodded. "It was so sweet and cuddly. It would be nice to have a kitten running around the Ruby Palace, don't you think?"

Hapgood nodded. "It would."

When they reached the wagon, Roxanne noticed one basket they had forgotten to deliver.

"This basket is for the Treetoppers at Sky Crest," Roxanne said. "That's very far away."

"I can fly this basket to Sky Crest," Hapgood said. "Why don't you return to the palace, Princess? It has been a long day, and you are probably tired.

Roxanne was a little tired. "All right," she said. "But be sure to stay away from the Mysterious Forest."

The Mysterious Forest was a dark strip of trees that separated the Red Mountains from other lands in the Jewel Kingdom. Princess Roxanne tried never to go into it. Bad things happened there.

"Don't worry about me," Hapgood replied. "I have Dragon sense. We Dragons always know when evil is near."

"What do you do then?" Roxanne asked as she handed him the basket.

"If we can't fight it, we call for help."

"How?" Roxanne asked. "With your ferocious roar?"

Roxanne had heard Hapgood roar a few times and knew how scary that could be.

"No, my lady, just the opposite," Hapgood said. "We sing the Dragon song."

"What's that?"

The Dragon hummed a few bars of a beautiful tune.

"Does it have words?" the princess asked.

"Sometimes," Hapgood replied. "But the words must come from the heart. And when this song is sung, no matter where I am, I will hear it."

Roxanne wanted to hear more but the light was fading. "You'd better hurry before it gets dark," she told her friend. "I wouldn't want you crashing into the mountains."

"Don't worry, my lady," Hapgood said

as he unfolded his wings and prepared to fly.

"Don't tell me you have Dragon vision, too?"

"No." Hapgood chuckled. "I was going to say, I know the way."

"Oh." Roxanne gave her friend a hug. "Be careful."

With two flaps of his wings, the Dragon was in the air.

"Good-bye!" Roxanne waved to Hapgood. "Hurry home!"

The Ruby Princess backed down the path as she watched Hapgood disappear into the sky.

Suddenly she tripped over something in the middle of the path. Roxanne's feet flew into the air and she fell to the ground.

"What was that?" she muttered, slowly raising her head. There in the middle of

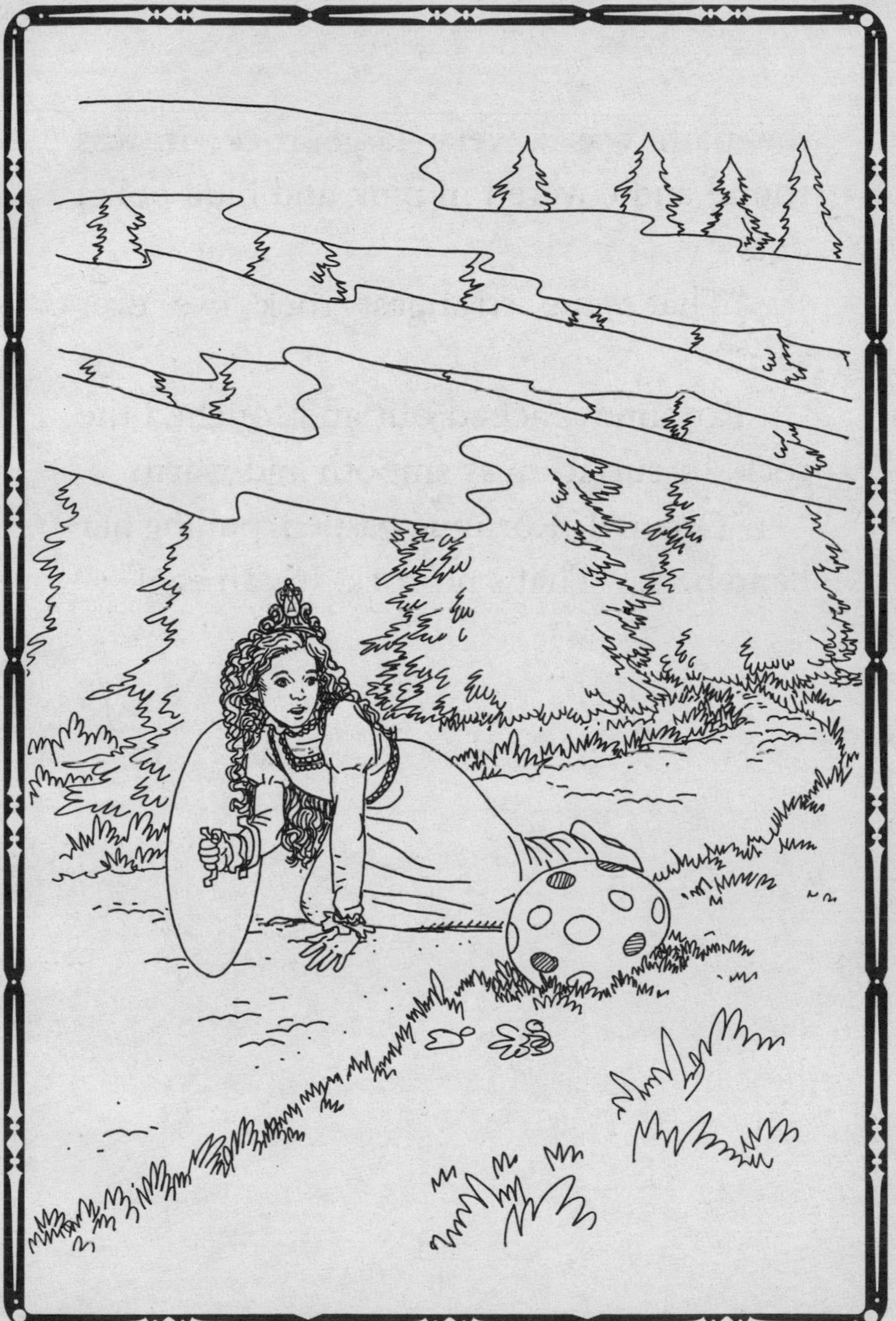

the path was a very large rock. It was round and covered in pink and blue polka dots.

"That's the strangest rock I've ever seen!"

Roxanne reached out and touched the rock. Its surface was smooth and warm.

"Oh, my!" Roxanne gasped, pulling her hand back. "That's no rock. It's an egg!"

Sassafras Is Born

The Ruby Princess searched the forest for a nest big enough to hold such a large egg.

Roxanne didn't see one in the treetops. And she didn't see one in the thicket around the tree trunks.

She knelt on the path beside the egg and patted its shell. "I'm sorry, Egg, but I don't know where you belong."

The egg rolled forward and bumped into her knee.

"What?" Roxanne gasped. "You didn't hear me, did you?"

The pink-and-blue egg wiggled back and forth.

Roxanne's eyes were huge. The egg seemed to be trying to tell her something. "Do you want me to take you home?" she whispered.

The egg jiggled again.

The princess swallowed hard. "Well, all right, then."

Roxanne made a little nest inside the wooden wagon out of pine needles and soft moss. Then the princess lifted the egg into the wagon. It was very heavy. Finally she covered the egg with her red velvet cape to keep it warm.

The Ruby Princess pulled the wagon

all the way to the Ruby Palace. When she reached the gates Roxanne shouted, "Clove! Nutmeg! Come help me!"

Seconds later a large Craghopper appeared at the front entrance. Clove had curly horns and hooves like a goat. She was the cook at the Ruby Palace. Her apron was covered in flour. Behind Clove stood her helper, a young Gnome named Nutmeg.

"Welcome home, Princess," Clove called. "What have you got there?"

Roxanne lifted the cape and showed Clove the pink-and-blue egg.

"That is the biggest egg I have ever seen," Clove declared. "It will make an omelette big enough to feed the entire palace."

Roxanne was certain she saw the egg jump. She put her hand on its shell and said, "No, Clove, you don't understand. This egg isn't for eating. I think there is a baby inside."

The Craghopper stared at the polka-dotted egg. "A baby what?" she finally asked.

Roxanne shrugged. "I'm not really sure."

"It has to be a bird," Nutmeg declared. "All baby birds come from eggs."

"But what kind of bird?" Roxanne wondered. "It would have to be a very big one. Maybe it is a Krok. That is the biggest bird in the Jewel Kingdom."

Clove shook her head. "Krok eggs are green. This egg is pink and blue."

Roxanne stared down at the egg. It was shaking.

"This egg is cold," the princess

announced. "We need to take it inside and keep it warm."

Clove called for Gruff, the palace guard, to help Princess Roxanne carry the egg into the palace. Roxanne made a nest for the egg in the center of her bed.

"Are you sure you want to do that?" Clove asked. "After all, you don't know what may come bursting out of that egg."

Roxanne nodded firmly. "I want this egg to feel completely at home in the Ruby Palace. My bed is the softest, warmest place I know."

Her bed sat on a raised platform in front of a big stone fireplace. The mattress was covered in a thick down comforter and had lots of fluffy pillows. Heavy red-and-gold velvet curtains hung down on either side.

"This is your own little nest," Roxanne whispered to the egg as she cradled it with pillows. "Welcome home."

Just then she heard a loud *Crack*!

A thin line cut across the top of the eggshell.

"It's hatching!" Roxanne cried. "My eggs is hatching!"

Clove, Nutmeg, and Gruff came running. All of them huddled around the bed to watch.

"I still think it's a bird," Nutmeg whispered as the crack got bigger and bigger.

Suddenly a hole appeared in the side of the egg. Then a big blue nose poked out of the hole.

"Look!" Gruff cried. "That's not a bird beak. That's a nose."

The hole grew wider and a large blue eye peeked through the opening.

"It is looking right at us," Roxanne whispered.

The eye disappeared and they heard a loud crunching sound. Suddenly a head with two fuzzy purple horns popped out of the egg.

"It's a cow!" Nutmeg declared.

"Stuff and nonsense," Clove sniffed. "Cows don't hatch out of eggs."

Crack!

The rest of the shell split apart and a pink-and-blue creature was born. He had a long scaly tail with purple spikes, a golden chest, and two tiny little golden wings.

"It's a Dragon!" Roxanne gasped.

Clove was grinning from horn to horn.

"This is a rare occasion. A very rare occasion indeed."

The baby Dragon blinked at the creatures looking down at him. Then his gaze fell on Roxanne. His big blue eyes lit up and he cooed, "Sass-a-fwas!"

Roxanne giggled. "Sassafras. Is that your name?"

The little Dragon chirped a happy squeak.

"Sassafras!" Roxanne repeated. "This baby's name is Sassafras."

On hearing his name, the baby Dragon toddled across the bed and buried his head in Roxanne's shoulder.

The Ruby Princess wrapped her arms around Sassafras.

It was love at first sight.

Sassy Meets the Sisters

———◆◆◆———

Roxanne was so excited about the birth of Sassafras that she sent invitations to her sisters. "Come meet Sassafras," the invitation read. "He's my baby Dragon."

None of the Jewel Princesses had ever seen a baby Dragon. They hurried as quickly as they could to the Red Mountains. And each princess brought

Sassafras a special gift from her kingdom.

They gathered in the garden of the Ruby Palace to give their presents to the little Dragon.

Emily, the Emerald Princess, brought a large wooden rattle carved from a limb of the Great Oak, in the Greenwood.

"I don't know what Dragons like," she said as she handed Sassafras the rattle. "But I know babies love rattles."

Sassafras shook the rattle with his pink-and-blue claw. He squeaked with delight.

"The Water Sprites in Blue Lake made this bonnet," Sabrina, the Sapphire Princess, said. "It was woven from the flax that grows by Bluebonnet Falls."

Roxanne put the bonnet on the Dragon's head and tied it under his chin. "Don't you look cute?" she cooed.

The baby Dragon chirped.

The Sapphire Princess tickled Sassafras, and the Dragon rolled on his back, kicking and giggling.

"He acts just like a little baby," Emily laughed.

"A very big baby," Roxanne corrected.

Demetra, the Diamond Princess, presented Sassafras with a bottle carved from a rare crystal found only in the White Winterland. "Here, little Sassy," she said. "Drink your milk from this."

Sassafras took the bottle in both claws and raised it to his mouth. After taking a long drink, he cried, "Goo!"

"Did you hear that?" Roxanne said to Demetra. "Sassy says the milk is *goo*."

Demetra tossed her long brown braid over one shoulder and smiled. "All babies think milk is *goo*."

"What else do you feed him?" Sabrina asked.

Roxanne frowned. "I'm not really sure. I guess he'll eat what Hapgood eats."

"Where *is* Hapgood?" Demetra asked. "I haven't seen him anywhere."

"He flew to Sky Crest yesterday to deliver the baskets to the Treetoppers," Roxanne explained. "I can't wait for him to come home and meet Sassy. He'll be so pleased." Roxanne tickled Sassy under the chin. "You'll love Happy. He's a genuine Dragon, just like you."

Sassy seemed to understand her. With a happy snort, he blew two pink puffs of smoke into the air.

Roxanne hugged the baby Dragon. "You are too cute!"

Suddenly a big shadow moved across the garden.

Emily looked up and cried, "Look, Roxanne. Hapgood's back."

Roxanne watched the Dragon circle far above their heads. Then she clapped her hands together. "I have an idea," she whispered. "Let's surprise Happy. Let's hide Sassafras."

"What fun!" Emily declared.

Roxanne had her sisters form a straight line in front of the fountain. Then she hid Sassafras behind them.

"Stand close together," she said. "And don't laugh."

"We promise," they said, trying to keep straight faces.

"And that goes for you, too, Sassy!" Roxanne called to the Dragon. "Be good!"

"Goo!" the baby Dragon squeaked.

Hapgood had landed by the palace

gates and was making his way to the garden.

"Hapgood!" Roxanne cried, running to meet her friend. "Have I got a surprise for you!"

"I love surprises." The big Dragon chuckled as she grabbed him by his claw and pulled him toward her sisters.

"Now, close your eyes," the princess instructed. "And don't peek."

"Very well, my lady." Hapgood did as he was told.

Roxanne waved one hand in front of his closed eyes to make sure he wasn't looking. "One . . . two . . . three!"

The princesses jumped apart to reveal the little pink-and-blue Dragon.

Hapgood opened his eyes and gasped.

"Happy, I want you to meet Sassy!" Roxanne cried. "Isn't this wonderful?"

The great Dragon's blue eyes turned a dark shade of purple. Red-and-yellow smoke poured from his nostrils.

"No, Princess," Hapgood boomed. "This is *not* wonderful. This is a disaster!"

Too Many Dragons!

 Princess Roxanne was very surprised. She asked her sisters to watch Sassafras while she took Hapgood to the corner of the garden to talk.

"Hapgood, what's the matter?" she asked as soon as they were alone. "I thought you would like the baby Dragon."

Hapgood took a deep breath. "Of

course I like that baby Dragon. I just don't understand what he is doing here."

Roxanne shrugged. "I found his egg in the middle of the forest. It was abandoned."

"The egg was *not* abandoned," Hapgood shot back. "We Dragons never leave our young."

Roxanne folded her arms across her chest. "Then what was the egg doing there?"

Hapgood shook his head. "It must have been an accident. The egg must have rolled out of the Valley of the Dragons."

Roxanne had heard stories of the Valley of the Dragons. But she had never seen it. The valley lay covered in a mist that protected it from the eyes of the world.

"Now that the egg has hatched," Hapgood continued, "the baby must go back to the valley. All Dragons grow up there."

"But Sassafras is very happy here," Roxanne protested. "He doesn't need to go back to some mysterious valley that can't keep track of its eggs."

"Excuse me, Princess," Hapgood said. "But you don't really understand how delicate a Dragon can be."

"Delicate?" Roxanne looked over her shoulder at Sassafras. He was galloping across the garden, playing a game of tag with her sisters. He didn't seem delicate at all.

"It can take hundreds of years for a Dragon egg to hatch," Hapgood explained. "If it does hatch."

"If?" Roxanne repeated. "Why if?"

"So much can happen to an egg over so

many years," Hapgood replied. "After a Dragon is born it must live in the special mist of the Valley of the Dragons until it is ready to go out into the world. And that takes years, too."

"Did you grow up in the Valley of the Dragons?" Roxanne asked.

"Oh, my, yes!" Hapgood nodded. "I was nearly fifty years old before I could breathe fire, and then another fifty years passed before I could fly. It took that long to learn my magic skills. And, of course, there were the other powers — invisibility and the Dragon song."

"But Sassafras can learn all of that here at the Ruby Palace," Roxanne said. "You can teach him, Hapgood."

Hapgood paced impatiently in a circle. "You still don't understand. It is the magical mist that gives us our powers and our strength. Sassafras must live in the safety of the mist if he is to grow up."

"But I want Sassafras to stay with me," Roxanne said stubbornly.

Smoke poured from Hapgood's nostrils. "Princess, please don't be selfish. If you keep that baby Dragon here with you, he will get sick. His color will change. His personality will change. It will be terrible. You must listen to me."

Roxanne looked back at the little Dragon. Sassafras had hopped into the fountain and was spraying the other princesses with water. He was so alive and healthy. He didn't seem to need that Dragon mist. Maybe Hapgood wasn't telling the whole truth.

Roxanne narrowed her eyes at Hapgood. "Are you sure I'm the one being

selfish? Maybe it's you. Maybe you don't want another Dragon at the Ruby Palace."

Hapgood's eye widened and he raised up to his full height. "How could you say that?" he bellowed so loudly that all of the Jewel Princesses came running to see what was the matter.

"Roxanne!" Demetra cried. "Are you all right?"

"I'm fine," Roxanne replied. "But I think something is the matter with Hapgood. He wants to give Sassafras away."

"What?" her sisters gasped.

"But why, Hapgood?" Sabrina asked. "He isn't hurting anyone."

Hapgood stared long and hard at the Ruby Princess. Finally he said, "If Princess Roxanne will tell you all that I have told her, you will understand."

Roxanne turned her back on Hapgood and ran to hug the baby Dragon. "You're staying with me."

Hapgood was angry. Little bolts of fire shot out of his nostrils. But he didn't say a word. Instead, he spread his huge wings and took to the sky.

As Roxanne watched Hapgood fly away, she whispered to Sassafras, "Don't worry, Sassy, he's just jealous. He'll come back, and we'll be one big happy family."

What's Wrong with Sassy?

Two days had passed since Hapgood flew away. All day long Roxanne had watched the sky, waiting for his return. But there was no sign of the big green Dragon.

Even Sassy seemed upset. He moped around the garden. He did not want to run or play. His bright pink-and-blue skin was beginning to fade.

"Sassy doesn't look very well," Demetra said to Roxanne that afternoon. "He hasn't eaten a thing, and he won't even look at the bottle I gave him."

Roxanne was worried, too, but she didn't want to admit it. "Sassy is fine," she said. "He's just missing Hapgood."

"You never told us why Hapgood was so upset," Sabrina said.

Roxanne waved one hand. "We just had a little fight, that's all."

Emily had tried to get Sassy to play with his rattle but he wasn't interested. "Sassy doesn't make those funny squeaks anymore," she said. "I just brought him inside to rest on his baby bed."

Roxanne hurried to the bed. The Dragon's color was even paler than before. She had to face the truth. Her little Dragon was sick.

"We have to call a doctor," Roxanne told her sisters.

"I hope you don't mind," Emily said. "But I sent for Nana Woodbine this morning. I thought Sassafras was looking ill even then."

Nana Woodbine lived in the Greenwood. She had great healing powers. Her mother was half Fairy and her father was a Wizard.

"Thank you for calling Nana," Roxanne said, squeezing Emily's hand. "We all want Sassy to get better."

The warm afternoon sun was starting to fade. Roxanne decided it would be best to move Sassy's bed beside the fire in the Great Hall.

Sassy nuzzled Roxanne's cheek with his nose. "Goo!" he said. He was asleep by the time Nana Woodbine arrived.

Nana was a pretty little woman with silver hair and big blue-green eyes. She peered at Sassy through gold-rimmed glasses.

"This little Dragon is sick," Nana told Princess Roxanne. "But Hapgood should know how to cure him."

Roxanne stared at the ground. "Hapgood isn't here," she murmured. "He, um, flew away."

Nana put her hand on Sassy's forehead. "His color isn't good. His skin feels cold and clammy. It should be warm," she said. "And his breathing is raspy."

"Can you help him?" Roxanne asked in a very worried voice.

"I'll try," Nana said, looking into her tapestry bag full of medicines. "But I've never taken care of a baby Dragon. I don't think I've ever seen one before."

"Really?" Roxanne asked.

"Oh, yes," Nana replied. "They usually stay hidden in their valley until they're much older."

Nana rummaged through her bag. "I could try some wisteria cream for his skin. And maybe some honeysuckle tea for his breathing. But I don't know what I can give for his color. It just seems to be fading away."

Roxanne barely heard Nana. She knew the herbs might help Sassy, but they wouldn't cure him. Hapgood had said Sassy would look and act this way if he was kept away from the mist. But she had refused to listen. Now there was only one thing Roxanne could do to help the baby Dragon.

"I have to take you back to the Valley of the Dragons," Roxanne whispered to Sassy. "Before it's too late."

She waited until Nana and her sisters left the room. Then the Ruby Princess wrapped Sassafras in a blanket and lifted him into the little wooden wagon.

She didn't know exactly where to find the Valley of the Dragons. But she knew that the entrance had to be near the spot where she had found the egg. Hapgood himself had said the egg rolled out of the valley.

"We'll go back to the forest," she told Sassy. "And then I'll help you find your way home."

The Dragon Song

"This looks like the spot where I found you," Roxanne said as she pulled Sassy up the mountain path in the wagon. "I remember there were lots of trees and some very large rocks."

"Goo," Sassy whispered.

Roxanne dropped the handle of the little wagon and huffed, "But practically every place in the Red Mountains has trees and large rocks."

Shielding her eyes with one hand, Roxanne looked up at the misty mountains where the sun was just starting to set. "The Valley of the Dragons must be up there somewhere. I'll bet your egg accidentally rolled down the mountainside and stopped here."

Sassy didn't reply. He just looked at her with his big blue eyes.

Roxanne had looped a leather bag with a compass and a map of her kingdom over her shoulder. She rolled out the map on the ground and tried to find their location.

"We're here, near Gnome's Notch." She looked up at the jagged row of mountain peaks. "We're going to have to climb over the Great Wall if we want to find any valleys."

"Goo," Sassafras cooed once more.

Roxanne knew she wouldn't be able to pull a wagon over the Great Wall. She was going to have to carry the baby Dragon.

"Come on, Sassy," she said, lifting him out of the wagon. "Let's go find your home."

Sassy whimpered. He looked even sicker than he had before.

Now the Ruby Princess knew she would have to move fast. Night was falling. Luckily a full moon was already rising.

Carrying Sassy on her hip, Roxanne worked her way up the rocky red peak. After hiking for nearly an hour she was out of breath. Sassafras had squeaked a few times when they started the climb, but he had been silent since then.

"Let's rest here," Roxanne finally said. "I'll bet you could use some water."

She pulled his bottle out of her bag, but Sassafras wouldn't drink. Roxanne tried to get him to eat a cracker, but he wouldn't even taste it.

Roxanne looked at the rocks and bushes above. They glowed a strange silver color in the moonlight. She scanned the Great Wall. There was no sign of a valley.

"We don't seem to be any closer to the Valley of the Dragons than we were before," she said miserably.

Sassafras rubbed his nose against her cheek. Roxanne was very worried. Sassafras looked worse than ever.

"If only Hapgood were here!" she moaned. "He'd know what to do."

At that moment a large Krok flew very near the mountain crag. Roxanne recognized the bird and leaped to her feet.

"Yoo-hoo! Goswald! Over here!" she

cried, cupping her hands around her mouth. "Help me! Please!"

The Krok looked down with a start. "Princess Roxanne," Goswald gasped. The big orange bird circled back and glided onto a large rock near the princess. "What are you doing here at this time of night?"

Roxanne gestured to Sassafras. "This little Dragon is sick. I'm trying to find the Valley of the Dragons. Do you know where it is?"

The bird swept one wing toward the jagged mountains. "It is out there somewhere. But the Valley of the Dragons hides in a magical mist. I don't know how to find it."

"Oh." Roxanne's shoulders sagged. "If I could just find Hapgood, he'd take us to the valley. Could you help me look for him?"

The orange bird nodded. "I'll try, but it is after dark and difficult to see."

"Oh, thank you," Roxanne cried. "All you have to do is circle the Red Mountains and call Hapgood's name. You're sure to see him. A great big Dragon is very hard to miss."

"I'll do my best," the bird said, lifting into the air. Roxanne watched the Krok fly off, then turned to Sassy and said, "Don't worry, little baby, help is on the way."

The two of them waited. And waited. Several more hours passed before Goswald returned. Unfortunately he was alone.

Roxanne's heart sank.

"Couldn't you find Hapgood?" Roxanne asked.

The big orange bird shook his head. "I looked everywhere, Princess, but he could be in a cave or hidden by rocks. After all, most creatures are asleep right now."

"Please keep looking, Goswald," Roxanne pleaded.

"Of course, my lady," the bird said, and flew away again.

The night was cold. Roxanne wrapped her blanket tighter around Sassafras. In the moonlight she could see that his color was paler than ever.

"Oh, Sassy," she said with tears in her eyes. "I am such a selfish princess. I wanted you all for my own, and look what I've done to you. I am so sorry."

Sassy nuzzled her cheek again.

"Go to sleep, my baby Dragon," she murmured. "And I'll sing you a song Hapgood taught me."

Sassafras perked up as she began to hum the melody.

"You like that?" Roxanne petted the

Dragon's fuzzy purple horns. "Of course you would. It's the Dragon song."

Roxanne's eyes popped wide open.

"That's it!" she cried. "I'll sing the Dragon song! Hapgood will be sure to hear it."

She closed her eyes and sang with all her heart. The words came to her like magic.

"Dragon, Dragon in the night.
Let us see your inner light.
Dragon with your heart so true
Hear my words and answer do."

Each note was filled with love for Sassafras and her old friend Hapgood.

Sassy listened and even cooed along in a few places. His color seemed to grow brighter.

When the Dragon song was done,

Roxanne searched the sky for Hapgood's familiar shape. But no one was there.

A large tear slipped down her cheek. "That song was my last hope," the Ruby Princess whispered to the baby Dragon. "Now I don't know what to do."

Roxanne closed her eyes and hugged Sassy as she began to cry.

It was nearly dawn when Roxanne heard a strange sound above her.

Whoosh. Whoosh.

Roxanne's eyes popped open. Could it be?

Whoosh. Whoosh.

The sound was closer and much louder.

The princess tilted her head back as a huge shadow covered the side of the mountain.

"Happy!" Roxanne cried with joy. "You found us!"

The Valley of the Dragons

 Princess Roxanne had never been so happy to see anyone in her life.

"You heard me!" she cried. "You heard the Dragon song."

Hapgood folded his wings into his body. "Yes, my princess," he said. "I listened with my heart, and heard."

Roxanne looked down at the baby Dragon. "Sassafras is sick," she whispered to Hapgood. "You were right and I was so wrong."

Hapgood raised one claw. "Let's not worry about that. All that matters is this little Dragon."

Roxanne nodded. "He needs to go back to his valley, but I can't find it."

The big green Dragon knelt down. "Climb onto my back and I'll take you there. It's just over that ridge."

"Where?" she asked as she lifted Sassafras onto Hapgood's back. "I don't see anything."

"That's because you're looking but not seeing," Hapgood replied. "Try it again and see with your heart."

Roxanne looked at the ridge once more. The sun was just rising and it was covered in a strange yellow mist. Roxanne took a deep breath and thought of the love she felt for Sassafras. Suddenly the mist that covered the top of the ridge cleared.

She saw green grass and sunshine. "I see it," she gasped. "I see the Valley of the Dragons."

"I believe you do." Hapgood chuckled. "Quickly, my lady. Let's fly there."

Roxanne wrapped her arms around Sassafras. "Hang on, little fellow. You're almost home."

With two flaps of his wings, Hapgood was in the air. He flew in a wide circle.

"Look!" Roxanne pointed to a little cottage tucked into the mountainside below. "I can see Applesap and Marigold's home. They must be just waking up. Good morning!" she cried. "Good morning, you two!"

The Dragon turned toward the rocky ridge. They flew over several more cottages, past a stand of tall fir trees, and then darted into a space between two cliffs.

Instantly the air was filled with the smell of flowers. Roxanne took a deep breath. So did Sassafras.

"Goo!" he sighed.

"Yes." The princess giggled. "It smells delicious."

They glided through the mist into a lovely green valley. Purple lupine flowers were clustered next to pink-and-white lilies. Blue columbine dotted the hillside.

This was the Valley of the Dragons.

As Hapgood swooped in for a landing, he called, "Welcome, Princess Roxanne, to my home."

"Oh, Hapgood," Roxanne whispered, "your home is beautiful."

The Dragon set down in a small meadow of yellow flowers. Only an hour earlier, Sassafras could barely hold up his head. Now he leaped off Hapgood's back and toddled through the deep grass. He stopped to touch and sniff every rock, flower, and bush.

Roxanne watched Sassy with tears of happiness in her eyes. Already his color had changed. He was bright pink and blue again.

Suddenly, Sassy squealed and galloped into the meadow. "What's going on?" Roxanne cried.

Hapgood pointed to a clump of purple flowers where two creatures were hiding. One had a striped head and two yellow horns. The other was the same colors as Sassy.

"Are those Dragons?" Roxanne gasped. "Baby Dragons?"

The two little Dragons jumped out of

the flowers and pounced on Sassafras. Sassy giggled as they rolled like puppies on the grass.

"They're adorable!" Roxanne cried, looping her arm over Hapgood's wing. "Look, Hapgood! Sassy has made some friends!"

"Yes," Hapgood said, smiling at the princess. "Our wandering Dragon is back where he belongs."

The Blue Hugaboo

 A week had passed since Princess Roxanne said good-bye to Sassafras. But she still missed him terribly.

Her sisters tried to cheer her up, but everything made Roxanne think of Sassy. In her bedroom was his little bed. In the garden she found his rattle. Sassy's bottle was still in the kitchen.

"I know he belongs in the Valley of the

Dragons," Roxanne told Princess Sabrina. "But I'm lonely without him."

"Please don't be lonely," the Sapphire Princess said. "I'm here with you."

Roxanne squeezed Sabrina's hand. "Thanks, but you're my sister. You don't need me to take care of you. I liked taking care of Sassy. It was fun giving him his bottle and playing with him in the garden."

"The garden!" Sabrina put her hands to her face. "Oh, my goodness. I almost forgot!"

Sabrina ran to the window of Roxanne's bedroom.

"What are you looking at?" Roxanne asked.

"The garden!"

Sabrina grabbed Roxanne by the hand and led her out into the hall. As they hurried down the long flight of stairs, Sabrina said, "Hapgood sent me to get you. Then we started talking and I just forgot. I hope it's not too late."

Roxanne stumbled after her sister. "Too late for what?"

Sabrina pulled Roxanne out the back door and pointed toward the fountain. "That."

Sitting in front of the fountain was a very large box with a big red ribbon on top. Roxanne stared at it curiously. It seemed to be hopping toward her.

"W-w-what is in the box?" Roxanne stammered.

Sabrina gave Roxanne a gentle push. "Go and see."

Roxanne tiptoed toward the mysterious box. It scooted toward her.

When she got close enough, she tugged on the red ribbon. It came untied instantly.

Suddenly the lid flipped off and a pair of fuzzy blue ears appeared. Two big brown eyes peeked out at her.

Roxanne leaned forward and two soft, furry paws wrapped around her neck. "Whirrrrr!" the little creature purred.

The little blue ball of fur looked like a teddy bear, except it had pointy ears and a small bump of a nose. It hopped into her arms and buried its soft furry face in her shoulder.

"Well, hello there, little fellow," Roxanne murmured. "What are you? And where did you come from?"

"He's a Hugaboo," a deep voice answered. "And he's a gift from me."

Roxanne turned to see Hapgood

peeking out from behind an elm tree. He was grinning from ear to ear. "Do you like him?"

Roxanne looked from the cuddly blue Hugaboo to the big green Dragon, and back again. "Like him?" she cried. "I love him!"

The Hugaboo heard her and clapped his paws together.

"Oh, Hapgood, thank you," Roxanne said, tickling the Hugaboo under his chin. "But why did you bring me a present?"

"Because you saved a baby Dragon's life," Hapgood said quietly.

"If I had listened to you, he wouldn't have needed saving," Roxanne confessed.

"True," Hapgood said, raising one eyebrow. "But you are young and are learning to listen."

Roxanne smiled up at her friend and once more thought of Sassafras.

She knew the next time she saw Sassy, he would probably be big and strong like Hapgood. But in her heart, he would always be her pink-and-blue baby Dragon.

About the Authors

JAHNNA N. MALCOLM stands for Jahnna "and" Malcolm. Jahnna Beecham and Malcolm Hillgartner are married and write together. They have written over seventy books for kids. Jahnna N. Malcolm have written about ballerinas, horses, ghosts, singing cowgirls, and green slime.

Before Jahnna and Malcolm wrote books, they were actors. They met on the stage where Malcolm was playing a prince. And they were married on the stage where Jahnna was playing a princess.

Now they have their own little prince and princess: Dash and Skye. They all live in Ashland, Oregon, with their big red dog, Ruby, and their fluffy little white dog, Clarence.

Visit the authors' Web site at http://www.jewelkingdom.com.